"Dad, I bet you thought you'd never see this book again," Julia Sandback said. "But when I came across this first edition of *Foul-up at the Floss Factory,* I knew you should have it."

Julia handed the pretty wood box to Mr. Sandback.

"What!" he sputtered, staring at the box. Then he grinned from ear to ear. "What a wonderful gift!"

He flung the box open. Eagerly, he peered inside. Then his face wrinkled into a puzzled frown.

Julia peeked into the box, too. Then she gasped.

"The book!" she cried. "It's gone!"

The Nancy Drew Notebooks

Available from Simon & Schuster

THE
NANCY DREW
NOTEBOOKS®

#47

The Crook Who Took the Book

CAROLYN KEENE
ILLUSTRATED BY JAN NAIMO JONES

Aladdin Paperbacks
New York London Toronto Sydney Singapore

First Aladdin Paperbacks edition April 2002

Copyright © 2002 by Simon & Schuster, Inc.

ALADDIN PAPERBACKS
An imprint of Simon & Schuster
Children's Publishing Division
1230 Avenue of the Americas
New York, NY 10020

The text of this book was set in Excelsior.

Printed in the United States of America
10 9 8 7 6 5 4 3 2 1

Library of Congress Control Number: 2001098779

NANCY DREW and THE NANCY DREW NOTEBOOKS
are registered trademarks of Simon & Schuster, Inc.

ISBN 0-7434-3761-6

1

Big Book News

"Fridays are the coolest," Nancy Drew said. Her third-grade class was walking in single file through the hall of their school, Carl Sandburg Elementary.

In front of Nancy marched her best friend George Fayne. George's real name was Georgia, but she hated to be called that. Behind Nancy was her other best friend, Bess Marvin. Bess and George were cousins.

"I know," George whispered over her shoulder. "Friday is the day before Saturday. And Saturday means soccer."

"That's true," said Nancy, who was also on the soccer team. "But I love Friday because it's library day."

Just as she said this, their teacher, Mrs. Reynolds, brought the class to a halt in front of the library. Nancy peeked through the door and saw that Mrs. Apple's third graders were already inside.

"Now, class," Mrs. Reynolds announced. "Remember to keep your voices low while you choose your books. And at the end of our library time, Mrs. Goldstein has an announcement for us."

"Hmm," Nancy whispered to Bess as the class poured into the library. "I wonder what the news is."

"Well, *I* wonder if a new Susie book has come in," Bess said. She headed straight for the shelf where her favorite books were kept.

George plopped down on the floor to peer at the animal books.

Nancy wandered over to the mysteries. She pulled out a book called *Tick-Tock Went the Missing Clock*.

"This looks good," she murmured. Soon she'd forgotten all about Mrs. Goldstein's news. She'd lost herself in the story. It was about a detective who had to find a clock before it struck twelve—or else!

"Hey," George said, popping up at Nancy's shoulder. "Don't you get enough mysteries in real life? I can't believe you want to read them, too."

Nancy looked up and shrugged. "I guess I never get sick of solving mysteries," she said. Then she pointed to the book under George's arm. "What did you get?"

"I found this neat book about giraffes," George said. "Did you know giraffes are related to camels?"

"Really?"

"And their tongues are black!" George said. "I'm not sure why. I guess I'll have to read the book to find out."

"Blech," said a squeaky voice.

Nancy and George turned to see Andy Nixon near the science-fiction shelf. Andy was in Mrs. Apple's class.

"Books are boring," Andy scoffed. "Unless they're comic books."

George rolled her eyes and muttered, "Boys."

"I have twenty-seven comic books at home," Andy said. "They're really old. I keep each one in its own plastic envelope so it won't get bent or dirty. My dad collects comic books, too."

"Isn't it hard to read a book that's in a plastic envelope?" Nancy said.

"That's the point," Andy said. "My comic books are totally special. My dad says they're collector's items. Someday I could sell them. Not that I'd want to. They're mine!"

"What good is a book if you don't read it?" Katie Zaleski piped up. She'd been listening in from a nearby section. "I'm going to be a writer when I grow up. My books will be so great, everyone will want to read them."

"Like Morton Sandback," Nancy said, nodding at Katie. "Every time one of his mysteries comes out, I just have to read it."

Just then Mrs. Goldstein, the librarian, walked up to them. Mrs. Goldstein had curly brown hair and hazel eyes. She was wearing a bright blue cardigan sweater.

"It's funny that you should mention

4

Morton Sandback, girls," she said. "I was just about to make an announcement about him."

Nancy gave a little hop of joy. She couldn't wait to hear the news.

Mrs. Goldstein raised a slender arm over her head and snapped her fingers. "Children, please finish choosing your books and gather around," she called. "I have some news."

All the third graders grabbed their books and crowded around Mrs. Goldstein.

"Who here has been to the Book Nook?" Mrs. Goldstein asked.

Bess, Nancy, George, and a bunch of the other kids raised their hands in the air.

"The Book Nook is the best," Nancy whispered to Bess. "What a great idea to put a bookstore in a big old house."

"A big, creepy house!" George said.

"Nuh-uh," Bess said. "I think the Book Nook is nice. I especially love the store mascot—Charlie the cat."

"Charlie?" Nancy asked. "He's the grouchiest cat ever. He never gets off his cat bed!"

"Well, he might be the grouchiest, but

he's also the prettiest," Bess said. "He's so white and fluffy."

"Does anybody know who owns the Book Nook?" Mrs. Goldstein asked.

"Sure," Mike Minelli said. "That tall, skinny lady with the red hair and freckles. She lives upstairs from the store."

Katie raised her hand. "I know the lady's name," she said. "It's Julia. She's really nice. Whenever I go to the Book Nook, she tells me about the latest books."

"You're right, Katie," Mrs. Goldstein said, smiling down at her. "But do you know Julia's last name? It's Sandback."

"Like . . . Morton Sandback?" Josie Blanton asked. She was one of Nancy's classmates.

"Yes," Mrs. Goldstein said. Her hazel eyes sparkled. "Julia Sandback is the daughter of Morton Sandback."

"Wow!" Katie sighed. "Julia's dad is a famous author!"

"As many of you know, Mr. Sandback has just published a new mystery called *Frogs, Dogs, and Mysterious Logs*," Mrs. Goldstein said.

Bess giggled. "What a funny title."

"Mr. Sandback also happens to be visiting his daughter for a week," Mrs. Goldstein continued. "So, as a treat, he's going to appear at the Book Nook this Sunday at noon. He'll answer questions and autograph copies of his books. This is a great opportunity, children. I know I'll be there."

"Me, too!" Nancy cried. Bess and George nodded excitedly.

The other kids were excited, too. Kyle Leddington turned to Orson Wong and said, "We should wear costumes on Sunday. I'll be a dog."

"I'll be a frog," Orson said. "Ribbit, ribbit." He jumped around wildly until he jumped right into Bess.

Bess rolled her eyes at Nancy. "Boys!"

"There's one more thing," Mrs. Goldstein said. "Julia has a special surprise for her father. She's come across a very rare copy of Mr. Sandback's first mystery, *Foul-up at the Floss Factory.*"

"What's so rare about it?" Katie asked. "I have that book at home."

"This is a first edition of the book," Mrs.

Goldstein said. "Most books are printed many times. But the first time is the most important. This first edition was published forty years ago, and only a few copies still exist. Even Mr. Sandback doesn't have one. So, Julia is going to present her father with the book."

Andy wasn't impressed.

"Too bad it's not a comic book," he said. "A first edition is really rare. That's what my dad says."

"Actually, Andy," Mrs. Goldstein said, "*Foul-up at the Floss Factory* is more like a comic book than you think. There's a picture on every page. The pictures are divided into boxes, just like a comic. That's called a graphic novel. You can see the story, as well as read it.

"In the back of the book, Mr. Sandback writes about reading comic books when he was a boy. Those comic books inspired him to write *Foul-up at the Floss Factory*."

"Well," Andy said, "it's still a book. And if it's a book, I don't like it."

2

Seeing Mr. Sandback

"**H**urry, Daddy," Nancy said, tugging at her father's hand. It was Sunday morning. Carson and Nancy Drew were walking to the Book Nook with Bess, Mrs. Marvin, and George.

"I don't want to be late to see Mr. Sandback," Nancy said.

"It's only eleven," Mr. Drew said, "and Mr. Sandback doesn't begin until noon. So, I think we're safe, Pudding Pie." That was one of Mr. Drew's pet names for Nancy. He tousled her reddish blond hair as he teased her.

"Sorry," Nancy said with a giggle. "I'm

just so excited to meet Mr. Sandback."

"I wonder what he's like," George said.

"Well, we'll find out soon," Mrs. Marvin announced as they reached the end of Drake Street. "Here we are!"

The girls gazed up at the Book Nook. It was in a house that was three stories high and painted several shades of blue. On the front porch were comfy wicker chairs and lots of flowering plants.

"I love coming to the Book Nook." Nancy sighed happily.

George pushed open the front door. It had a tinkling bell on the doorknob. "I like to pretend that all those skinny aisles between the bookshelves are secret passageways," she said.

"I'm going to say hi to Charlie," Bess called. She ran over to the store's front desk and peeked behind it.

Nancy followed her and took a peek, too. There was Charlie—a fat, fluffy, white cat with green eyes. As always, he was curled up on a plaid cat bed, looking grouchy.

Bess dropped to her knees. "He's so soooft," she cooed, stroking Charlie's thick fur.

"*Mrowr! Sssss,*" Charlie complained. Then he swiped at Bess with his claws.

"Eeek!" Bess cried, jumping backward.

"I don't know why you like that cat so much," George said. "He always tries to scratch you."

"And he *never* gets off that bed," Nancy said, "so you can't really play with him."

"*Sssss,*" Charlie hissed, squinting his green eyes at Bess.

"Um, maybe we should leave Charlie alone now," Nancy said. She grabbed Bess's arm to steer her away from the grumpy cat. Then she stopped in her tracks.

"Hey, the Book Nook is all changed around!" she exclaimed.

Usually bookshelves filled the first floor. Now a lot of them had been moved aside. In the center of the room stood a big wooden table stacked high with copies of Morton Sandback's latest book.

Facing the table were rows of folding chairs. A few people had already settled into their seats. Nancy saw that some of them were her classmates. Mrs. Goldstein, the school librarian, was there too.

"Why don't Mrs. Marvin and I save us some seats," Mr. Drew said. "You girls can look around. Just be back down here in a few minutes."

"Thanks, Daddy," Nancy said. Then she turned to Bess and George. "Let's go!"

The girls headed for the stairs. The second floor of the store had rooms for unusual old books. There was also a room for kids. It had books and music as well as stuffed animals and toys.

"Let's check out the stuffed animals," Bess said as they clomped up the steps.

"I think we should go to that dark room at the end of the hall," George said. "You know, the one with all the history books. That's the spookiest."

"Ooh, no!" Bess exclaimed as they reached the top of the stairs. "Too scary."

"Come on," George called. She dashed down the long, narrow hallway. "It'll be fun. We can play hide-and-seek." She headed into the last doorway on the left.

"Ready or not, here I come," Nancy called. She ran down the hallway, too, with Bess on her heels.

13

At the doorway to the history room, Nancy and Bess peeked inside. Nancy led Bess down one aisle of books. They turned left. Then right. Nancy found herself staring at a wall.

"Dead end!" she exclaimed.

"Where did George go?" Bess asked.

"George?" said a voice behind them.

Nancy and Bess spun around to see a young man in a brown T-shirt and worn corduroy pants. He had spiky black hair, and the nametag on his T-shirt said Anderson Quilling.

"Hi, Anderson," Nancy said.

Anderson Quilling worked at the Book Nook. He knew where to find any book in the cluttered store, and he seemed to know the name of every child who shopped there.

"I just saw George sneaking into the science room," Anderson said.

"Hey," George called from far away. Nancy peered across the hall. George was crawling out from behind a big chair. She came over to the history room doorway. "No fair, Anderson. You just gave me away."

Bess ran up to George and tagged her

shoulder. "You're it!" she announced.

"Oops," Anderson said with a guilty grin. "Hide-and-seek, huh? Sorry, I didn't know."

Bess pointed to a box tucked under Anderson's arm. "What's that?" she asked.

The box was rectangular and made of beautiful polished wood. It was exactly the color of caramel. Nancy saw a little silver lock on the lid.

"I can't tell you," Anderson said. "It's a surprise."

"Does it have to do with the rare book that Julia is giving to Mr. Sandback?" George asked excitedly.

Anderson's face fell. "Oh," he said. "I guess you already know."

"It's okay, Anderson," Nancy said. "Even though we know about the surprise, it's still exciting."

"Yes!" Anderson agreed. "A first edition of *Foul-up at the Floss Factory*. That's a big deal. You know, I'm trying to be a writer myself," he told the girls. "Maybe someday I'll have a book published, too."

Anderson heaved a big, sad sigh. Then he shook his head and tried to smile cheerily.

"Anyway," he said, "a book like *Foul-up* can't be presented in a plain cardboard box. So, Julia asked me to find a beautiful gift box."

"It *is* beautiful," Nancy said. She reached out to touch the smooth wood, but Anderson pulled the box away.

"Ah-ah-ah," he said. "Nobody gets to see this book until Mr. Sandback opens the box himself."

Nancy checked the clock on the history room wall. "Well, if we don't get downstairs," Nancy said, "the big surprise is going to be no seats."

A few minutes later Nancy and her friends were fidgeting in their chairs.

"I wish Mr. Sandback would get here already," Katie Zaleski said. She was sitting in front of Nancy. "I have so many questions to ask him."

Finally Julia Sandback stood up behind the wooden table. All the chattering kids and grown-ups fell silent.

"If you think it's fun to read a Morton Sandback mystery," Julia said to the group, "imagine what it was like growing up with

Morton Sandback as your father. My dad used to send my brothers and me on treasure hunts after dinner. The winner would get extra dessert."

"Ooh, good idea, Mom," Bess said. She prodded her mother with her elbow.

"My point is," Julia continued, "that my father believes that adventures aren't just for books. But see for yourself. Here he is—Morton Sandback!"

With that, Mr. Sandback walked into the room. He was as tall and skinny and red-headed as Julia. He was dressed in plaid trousers and a black vest covered with felt patches. Some of the patches looked like books. Others looked like pens and pencils. Some looked like typewriters.

The famous author peered at the audience over half-moon glasses. Then he broke into a big, friendly grin.

"Thank you, Julia," he said. "And hello there, kids. Let's jump right in. Who has a good, juicy question for me?"

"I do, I do," shouted a dozen kids, waving their hands. One of them was Nancy. But

Mr. Sandback pointed to someone sitting behind her.

"Mr. Sandback," said a squeaky voice.

Nancy twisted around in surprise. Andy Nixon was sitting right behind her, next to his dad. What was he doing here? He hated books!

"Which do you think is better?" Andy asked. "Comic books or book-books?"

Mr. Sandback laughed. "I guess most writers would say, 'book-books,'" he said. "But I grew up reading comic books. I think they're great. I even tried to make some of my early books seem like comic books."

"You mean graphic novels?" Andy asked.

"Exactly," Mr. Sandback said. "I'm impressed that you know that."

"Only because Mrs. Goldstein told us," George whispered to Nancy and Bess. "Remember, she said *Foul-up at the Floss Factory* was a graphic novel."

"Shh," Andy whispered. "I can't hear Mr. Sandback!"

"And guess what?" Mr. Sandback said. "I think that if I hadn't read comics as a kid, perhaps I wouldn't be an author today."

Next Mr. Sandback called on Katie Zaleski.

"How do I become a famous writer like you?" she asked.

"I don't know about the famous part," Mr. Sandback replied, "but I can tell you what to do if you want to be a writer. Just read as many books as you can. That's the best way to learn how to write."

The next question came from George. "Do you write on a computer?" she asked.

"Oh, I'm old-fashioned," Mr. Sandback replied with a smile. "I use good old number-two pencils to write my books."

Nancy thrust her hand in the air once more. This time Mr. Sandback pointed at her.

"Mr. Sandback," Nancy said, "how do you come up with all your mysteries?"

"Why, look around you, young lady," he said. "Life is filled with wonderful mysteries. They're everywhere. I just take the time to write them down."

"Cool!" Nancy whispered.

Many questions later Julia stepped to her father's side. "In a few minutes, Mr.

Sandback will autograph books for you. But first I have a special gift for my dad."

From behind her back Julia brought out the beautiful wooden box.

"That's the box Anderson had in the history room," Nancy whispered to Bess and George. "But where's Anderson?" Nancy looked around the crowded store. "I wonder why he didn't stay to see Mr. Sandback."

Julia held up the box. "Dad, I bet you thought you'd never see this book again," she said. "But when I came across this first edition of *Foul-up at the Floss Factory*, I knew you should have it." Then she handed the box to Mr. Sandback.

"What!" he sputtered, staring at the box. Then he grinned from ear to ear. "What a wonderful gift!"

He flung the box open. Eagerly, he peered inside. Then his face wrinkled into a puzzled frown.

Julia peeked into the box, too. Then she gasped.

"The book!" she cried. "It's gone!"

3

The Mystery of the Missing Mystery

The book has disappeared?" Nancy cried, turning to her father. "But what could have happened to it?"

"I don't know," Mr. Drew said. He looked concerned.

Julia was more than concerned. She was near tears. Nancy saw Mrs. Goldstein jump to her feet. She walked to the front of the room and put her hand on Julia's shoulder. She whispered something into Julia's ear.

Julia turned to the audience.

"Well, it appears we have a real-life mystery on our hands," she said. "While I get on the case, why don't you line up for Mr. Sandback's autograph."

Then she dashed into the back office with Mrs. Goldstein at her side.

Nancy and the other children lined up in front of the big table. Looking sad, Mr. Sandback uncapped a pen and took a book from the first child in line. As he was about to sign it, he paused. Then he looked up, and he spoke.

"I didn't realize how right I was when I said mysteries are all around us, children," he said. "But what I want to know is—are detectives all around us, too? Can any of you help me solve the mystery of the crook who took the book?"

Bess gasped and looked at Nancy. "You're a detective, Nancy," she said. "You have to help Mr. Sandback."

"Totally," Nancy said. "I'll talk to him when I get to the front of the line. I feel so bad for Mr. Sandback. Why would someone take his first edition?"

"And he's so nice, too," Bess said sadly. "He's just how you'd imagine Morton

23

Sandback should be. Right down to that funny vest with all the patches."

Nancy bit her lip and nodded in agreement.

It wasn't long before she herself was standing in front of Mr. Sandback. She handed him the copy of *Frogs, Dogs, and Mysterious Logs* that her father had bought for her.

"Ah," Mr. Sandback said, giving her a kind smile. "You're the young lady who was so interested in my mystery ideas."

"Yes," Nancy said. "I'm Nancy Drew. I'm a detective."

"Get out of here," Mr. Sandback said playfully.

"Uh-huh," Nancy said. "I have a clue book and everything. But I don't have it with me. I didn't expect to run into a mystery today."

"See, the missing book proved me right, Nancy," Mr. Sandback said. "We must always be ready for a mystery."

"Oh, I am," Nancy replied, sticking her chin in the air. "In fact, I'm going to do everything I can to help you find that book, Mr. Sandback."

"Why, thank you," Mr. Sandback said. "Lots of other kids want to help out, too. The more sleuths, the better! If you or any of your friends find any clues, you can reach me here at the bookstore. I'll be in town visiting with Julia for the rest of the week."

With that, Mr. Sandback opened Nancy's copy of *Frogs, Dogs, and Mysterious Logs*. He scribbled a message on the title page. Then he signed his name with big, loopy letters. He handed the book back to her and said, "Good luck, Nancy." Then he winked.

Nancy grinned back and walked to the front of the bookstore. Mr. Drew and Mrs. Marvin were waiting there.

"Let's see what Mr. Sandback wrote in your book," Mr. Drew said.

Nancy flipped open her book and read Mr. Sandback's message out loud: "'For Nancy Drew, a clever girl who, with a clue, just may unravel this mystery new. Best of luck, Morton Sandback.'"

"Cool," George said. She had just finished having her own book signed. "He wrote you a poem."

Nancy was inspired. "I say we get to work solving this mystery right now," she announced. "After all, we *are* at the scene of the crime."

"I'm sorry, Nancy," Mrs. Marvin said. "But Bess and George and I have to leave. We're having Sunday dinner with the girls' grandmother."

"Time to leave already?" George said. "But this is a big, important mystery. I want to help. I mean, the thief could be making a getaway right now!"

"Well, I'm sure Julia is doing everything she can," Mrs. Marvin said. "Why don't you girls and Nancy come here after school tomorrow. You can get started then."

"All right," George and Bess said together.

"Is that okay, Daddy?" Nancy asked her father as her friends waved goodbye.

"Sure, Pumpkin," Mr. Drew said. "Don't worry. I'm sure the mystery will keep until tomorrow. Now, let's head home ourselves. I've got to do some work. But then we'll have macaroni and cheese for dinner."

"With Hannah's apple pie for dessert?"

Nancy asked. Hannah Gruen was the Drews' housekeeper.

"You got it!" Mr. Drew answered with a laugh.

"Yum!" Nancy said. They headed for the door. Suddenly, something white and fluffy ran across Nancy's feet, almost tripping her.

"Whoa!" Nancy cried. "Hey, that's Charlie!" She watched in surprise as the grouchy cat darted across the bookstore.

"That's funny," Nancy said. "I thought Charlie *never* got off his bed." She glanced behind the front desk. Charlie's cat bed looked lumpy and messy.

"Then again, that bed doesn't look very comfortable," she said. "If I were Charlie, I'd take a hike, too."

Nancy shrugged and followed her dad out of the bookstore. As they began their walk home, Nancy frowned. Then she looked up at Mr. Drew.

"I wonder why someone would take Mr. Sandback's book," she said.

"No idea, Pudding Pie," Mr. Drew said. "What a shame."

"The thief would probably be someone who loves to read," Nancy said. "But that would make everybody who was at the Book Nook today a suspect. After all, they all love to read."

Except Andy Nixon, Nancy suddenly realized.

Andy hates books, Nancy thought. On the other hand, he seemed pretty excited about what Mr. Sandback was saying about graphic novels. Maybe Andy wants to add graphic novels to his comic book collection. And he's going to start with *Foul-up at the Floss Factory*!

This worried Nancy so much that she went straight to her room when she and her father arrived home. She opened her book bag and pulled out her shiny blue clue notebook. Turning to a crisp new page, she wrote, "The Mystery of the Missing Mystery."

Then she scribbled, "Suspect #1: Andy Nixon."

One Book Crook Gets Off the Hook

The next morning Nancy, George, and Bess were filing into school.

"How was dinner at your grandmother's?" Nancy asked.

"Great!" George said. "She made meatloaf with lots of ketchup."

"And strawberry shortcake for dessert," Bess added, rubbing her tummy.

"But the mystery's more important than our dinner," George said as the girls approached the school library. They had to pass the library to get to their classroom. "So, what do you think about Mr. Sandback's missing book, Nancy? Any suspects?"

"Well, there is one—" Nancy started to say. Then something caught her eye. Andy Nixon was standing at the library door. He was writing his name on the Internet sign-up sheet.

Every recess period two Carl Sandburg students were allowed to sign up for computer time in the library. Then Mrs. Goldstein would help them surf the Internet.

Nancy darted to Andy's side. She peeked over his shoulder at the sign-up sheet. Yes! The line next to his name was blank. Nobody else had signed up yet.

Andy finished writing his name and turned around. "Oh, hi, Nancy," he said. "I'm skipping recess today, and it's not just because I hate dodgeball. I have some very important research to do."

"What kind of research?" Nancy asked.

"Oh . . . just research," Andy said. Then he showed Nancy the back of his hand. "Check out my temporary tattoo. It's one of my favorite comic book heroes, Slugman!"

"Ewww!" Nancy squealed. "Good thing that tattoo washes off."

Andy gave her a funny look and headed down the hall.

Nancy sighed. "Why are my suspects always gross boys?" she whispered.

Then she remembered the Internet sign-up sheet. Nancy dug into her book bag for a pencil. She jotted her own name next to Andy's.

George and Bess ran up behind Nancy.

"What's going on?" Bess demanded. "Why did you dash off like that?"

George peered at the sign-up sheet. "You're skipping recess for computer time? But it's dodgeball day!"

"Do you see who else has signed up?" Nancy said.

"Andy Nixon," Bess read off the sheet.

"Make that Andy Nixon, chief suspect in the missing book mystery," Nancy whispered.

"Really?" George whispered. "You think Andy took the book?"

"I can't be sure yet," Nancy said. "But maybe at recess I'll find out."

Nancy sighed. The morning seemed endless! First Mrs. Reynolds had given the class a spelling quiz. Next they'd done

32

math worksheets. *Three* math worksheets.

Finally the bell rang for recess.

"Yay!" yelled most of the kids, popping out of their chairs and racing to the classroom door.

"Dodgeball day," Mike Minelli yelled. "My favorite!"

"Yuck," Bess said. "I'm jumping rope!"

Nancy didn't say a word. She just grabbed her clue notebook and hurried to the library. She didn't want to miss out on Andy Nixon's "research."

In the library Andy settled into the computer chair. Mrs. Goldstein stood at his side. Today her cardigan sweater had green and purple stripes. She turned to Nancy as she walked into the library.

"Hello, Nancy," she said. "Andy and I are just getting started. Would you like to look at a book while you wait?"

"Sure," Nancy said, grabbing the first book she saw. It was about antique cars. Bo-ring. But that didn't matter. Nancy wasn't *really* going to read the book. Instead, she was going to see what Andy was up to. She sat down in a chair near the computer and listened hard.

"So, what can I help you with, Andy?" Mrs. Goldstein asked.

"Can you help me find some graphic novels?" Andy said.

"Like *Foul-up at the Floss Factory*?" Mrs. Goldstein replied.

"Yup," Andy said. "I want to know if there are other books like that."

This proves it, Nancy thought as Mrs. Goldstein and Andy began pointing and clicking with the computer mouse. Andy must have stolen Mr. Sandback's book. Now he wants other graphic novels to add to his collection!

Click.

Click-click.

Click.

Nancy fidgeted. She pretended to read her antique car book while Mrs. Goldstein and Andy went from Web site to Web site.

Finally, Mrs. Goldstein said, "Well, we've found ten books, Andy. Would you like me to see if we have any of them here?"

"Yes, please," Andy said.

But as Mrs. Goldstein went to check on the books, Nancy peered around her chair. Andy looked a little sad. "What's wrong, Andy?" Nancy said.

"Well, those other graphic novels might be okay," he said, "but I bet they're not as cool as *Foul-up at the Floss Factory.*"

"Why do you say that?" Nancy said.

"Because Mr. Sandback was really neat," Andy said. "I bet that was a really great old book. And it's a collector's item! I hope you catch whoever snatched it."

Nancy's eyes widened. Mr. Sandback had turned Andy into a book lover! And a book lover would never steal a rare book. Andy seemed to be innocent after all.

Mrs. Goldstein returned, bringing Andy a small stack of graphic novels to check out.

"Thanks a lot, Mrs. Goldstein," he said. Then he looked at the library clock. "Recess isn't over yet? Ugh—I guess I'm going to play . . . dodgeball."

Andy slumped out of the library while Nancy bit her lip. Well, that's one suspect down the drain, she thought. But if Andy didn't steal *Foul-up at the Floss Factory,* who did?

"So, Nancy," Mrs. Goldstein said, turning to her with a kind smile. "Were you wondering about great books, too?"

Nancy gasped. Mrs. Goldstein's words had reminded her of something Anderson Quilling had said the day before: "I'm trying to be a writer myself. Maybe someday I'll have a book published." And he had looked really sad. Anderson dreamed of being an author just like Mr. Sandback.

Maybe, Nancy thought, Anderson is jealous of Mr. Sandback.

"Um, maybe I'll come back another day, Mrs. Goldstein," Nancy told the librarian.

Then Nancy opened her clue notebook. She crossed out Andy's name and wrote in: "Anderson Quilling—angry author?"

As she wrote it, Nancy felt bad. Anderson was really nice. She hated to think he had taken the book.

One thing's for sure, she thought. I need proof. And that means going back to the Book Nook with Bess and George!

5

The Book Man in the Basement

Just as Nancy closed her clue notebook, the bell rang. She hurried out of the library and headed to the cafeteria. She couldn't wait to tell Bess and George about Andy . . . and Anderson.

When Nancy arrived, Bess and George were already eating their lunches.

"I brought your lunch for you, Nancy," George said. She passed Nancy's pink-and-purple lunch sack across the table.

"Thanks," Nancy said. She opened her lunch and pulled out a tuna sandwich.

"So, what happened at the library?" Bess asked.

As she unwrapped her sandwich, Nancy told George and Bess everything that had happened with Andy and Mrs. Goldstein.

"You're right," George said when Nancy had finished her story. "It doesn't sound like Andy would steal Mr. Sandback's book."

"So now we're back to having no suspects," Bess wailed. She took a big bite of her peanut-butter-and-jelly sandwich.

"Well," Nancy started to say, "actually—"

"Yah!" Mike Minelli yelled. He plopped down on the bench next to Nancy. He waved his forearm in front of her face. There was an angry red scratch running across it.

"Ewww, gross, Mike!" Nancy squealed.

"Yeah!" Mike agreed. But Nancy knew that to him, gross was a good thing. "Charlie the cat gave it to me at the Book Nook yesterday. That's one mean cat!"

"He's not mean," Bess said. "He just doesn't like people to bother him when he's in his bed."

Nancy gasped.

"What is it, Nancy?" George asked. Mike

had already jumped up to go wave his icky scratch in someone else's face.

"I just thought of something," Nancy said. "Bess, George, I think we may have two new suspects. But we need more clues. Which means we have to head back to the Book Nook after school!"

Since they already had permission, Nancy, Bess, and George headed to the Book Nook as soon as the last bell rang. When they walked through the door, they saw Julia sitting at the front desk.

"Well, hello, girls," she said. "Back so soon?"

"We're here to help solve the mystery of the missing book," Nancy said. "Unless the book's been found already."

Julia's face fell. "No, I'm sorry to say there's been no sign of the book," she said. "What a disappointment. I so wanted my father to have it."

"Well, Julia," Nancy said, "I have a hunch. And if I'm right, that book is right under your nose!"

"What?" Julia said. She sounded surprised.

"Well, actually," Nancy said with a giggle, "it's right under Charlie the cat." She pointed at Charlie, who was curled up in his plaid bed, scowling.

"You think Charlie took the book?" Bess cried.

"No," Nancy said. "But maybe he has it. After the book disappeared, I noticed Charlie running away from his cat bed. And you know Charlie—"

"*Never* gets out of his bed," Bess finished.

"So, if someone wanted to hide Mr. Sandback's book," Nancy explained, "Charlie's bed would be the best place in the whole store."

"We just have to move Charlie so we can look," Bess said. She sounded scared.

"*Mrowr,*" the cat growled.

"This could get ugly," George said.

"Oh, Charlie," called a voice on the stairs behind them.

Nancy spun around. "Mr. Sandback!" she said. "Hello."

Mr. Sandback stood on the bottom step, grinning at the girls. "I heard what you said about your hunch, Nancy," he said. "I think

41

it's a good one. And I may be able to help."

He reached into his pocket and pulled out a catnip mouse. He walked over to Charlie's bed and dangled the mouse in front of the cat's nose. Then he tossed the toy a few feet away. Charlie meowed loudly and dashed after it.

Nancy pounced on the cat bed and lifted the bumpy plaid cushion. Nothing.

Nancy gazed up at Mr. Sandback sadly. "I guess my hunch was wrong," she said. "Which means . . ."

"What is it, Nancy?" Julia said.

"I have another hunch," Nancy said. She didn't want to tell Julia that she suspected Anderson. Not until she was sure. So she asked Julia a question instead.

"Can you tell me where you last saw the book before it disappeared?" Nancy said.

"It was in the wooden gift box that Anderson got for me," Julia said.

"Where's the box now?" Nancy asked.

"I put it in the storage room in the basement," Julia said. "Would you like to see it?"

"Yes, please," Nancy said.

The girls followed Julia to the back of the

bookshop and down a flight of narrow, rickety stairs.

"Ew, a spider web," Bess whispered.

"Shhh," George said. "It's no big deal."

Nancy shivered a bit as they headed into the damp basement. Julia led them into a big storage room. It was crowded with cartons, old books, and cast-off furniture.

"Now, where did I put that box?" she muttered. She began searching a cluttered shelf.

Tap. Taptaptaptap. Taptap.

Nancy picked up a flashlight and shone it into the shadowy corner of the storage room. "Anderson!" she said, with surprise.

Anderson Quilling was sitting at a desk in the corner, typing away on a big black typewriter. He was frowning at the page, and his hair looked messier than ever. But when he looked up and saw Nancy and her friends, he smiled.

"Oh, hello, girls," Anderson said. "This is where I do my writing. It's very quiet down here."

Julia turned from the shelf she was searching. "Anderson writes and writes and writes," she whispered to the girls. "But nobody will publish his books. But I have faith. I think he'll be a big success one day."

She turned back to the shelf. A moment later she cried out, "Here's the box!" She held out the brown box to the girls. "Look, the lock has been broken."

"May I see it, Julia?" Nancy asked.

"Of course." Julia handed the pretty polished box to Nancy. George and Bess crowded near to peer at the box, too.

"What are you looking for, Nancy?" Bess asked.

"I don't know, exactly," Nancy said with a shrug.

She looked at the box's bottom. Then she looked at the top and all around its sides. Finally Nancy fiddled with the broken lock and flipped the box open.

"Hmm," she said.

"What?" Bess, George, and Julia said together.

"Look at that," Nancy said. She pointed to the hinges that joined the lid to the box. "Something is caught here."

Nancy plucked a bit of fabric from the

hinge. "It looks like felt," she said, holding the scrap between her fingers. "Red felt." She looked at Julia. "Do you remember seeing this on the box before?" she asked.

Julia shook her head. "Let's ask Anderson." She took the scrap from Nancy and approached the store clerk.

"I hate to bother you, Anderson," Julia said, "but do you remember seeing this bit of felt in the box hinges when you picked it out yesterday?"

"No," Anderson said. "I don't think it was there when I gave you the box." Then he started typing again.

"Let's go upstairs, girls," Julia whispered. As they walked up the stairs, Nancy asked Julia another question.

"After Anderson gave you the box, what did you do with it?"

"Well, I checked to make sure the book was inside," Julia recalled. "Then I locked the box. And then I put it on a shelf beneath the cash register at the front desk."

"Hmm," Nancy said. "Can I hang on to that scrap of felt?"

"Sure, Nancy," Julia said. She handed over the fabric. "What do you think it is?"

"Maybe this felt was part of the thief's clothes," Nancy said. "And it got caught in the box hinges."

Silently, she was thinking one more thing: Maybe that thief was Anderson Quilling!

6

A Book Full of Clues

"Good thinking, Nancy," Julia said as they left the basement. "The red felt is a great piece of evidence."

When they reached the top of the stairs, the phone at the front desk was ringing.

"Excuse me," Julia said. She dashed away to answer it.

Nancy turned to George and Bess. "Do you remember if Anderson Quilling was wearing any red felt yesterday?" She whispered so no one would hear her.

"I don't know," George said. "I never notice clothes and stuff like that."

Bess tilted her head and thought hard. "I

think he was wearing lots of brown," she said.

"Julia said she left the box on a shelf under the front desk," Nancy whispered. "Anderson could have gotten to the box, broken the lock, and left with the book. That would explain why he wasn't at Mr. Sandback's appearance."

"Why would Anderson do that?" Bess asked.

Nancy glanced at Mr. Sandback. He was now sitting on an easy chair near the front desk. He had a small smile on his face. As soon as Julia hung up the phone, he stood up and turned to her.

"Oh, Julia," Mr. Sandback said. He draped his long, skinny frame over the counter. He had a glint in his eye. "I have an idea. Your shop clerk, Quilling. He's an odd fellow, isn't he? Perhaps he took my book?"

"Anderson?" Julia said. "Never! He's worked for me for years. I trust him completely."

"But," Mr. Sandback said, "isn't it poss—"

"Dad," Julia said, sounding exasperated. "It *isn't* possible. Anderson gave me the box. Then he left. I saw him drive away myself. And *then* I saw the book in the box and locked it. So, by the time the lock was broken and the book was stolen, Anderson was long gone."

"Oh," Nancy whispered to her friends. "I guess that rules out Anderson Quilling."

"Well, then who *is* it?" Bess practically shouted.

Julia and Mr. Sandback both jumped and looked in the girls' direction.

"Sorry," Nancy said. "We're just really frustrated by this mystery. I'd love to find that book for you. But all I have is one clue." She held up the scrap of red felt.

"You know," Mr. Sandback said, rubbing his chin slowly, "this reminds me of one of my own mysteries—*The Absent Award.*"

"I have that book at home," Nancy said excitedly.

"It's a story much like this one, isn't it?" Mr. Sandback said. "Except instead of an author being awarded with a rare book, an actor is given a trophy."

"But the award was stolen," Nancy said. "I remember. You had a really cool detective tracking down all these clues. It was a great book."

"Thank you," Mr. Sandback said. He walked back to the comfortable chair and sat down. He gave Nancy, Bess, and George another big smile.

"Who knows?" he said. "Maybe there are some clues to be found in that book."

"Uh, maybe," Nancy said. But inside, she wasn't so sure.

The Absent Award is just a story, she thought to herself. This is a real-life mystery. How can there be clues in a book?

As if he could read her mind, Mr. Sandback said, "Remember what I said yesterday, Nancy? Life is full of mysteries. And the solutions can be easy to find. You just have to know where to look. You have to pay attention to the hints that are dropped in your lap."

"Thanks for the advice," Nancy said. Now she was really confused. Talking to Mr. Sandback was a mystery in itself!

"And remember, don't lose that clue," Mr. Sandback said. He pointed at the bit of felt in Nancy's hand.

"That *is* good advice," Nancy said with a smile. She unzipped her book bag and pulled out her shiny blue clue notebook. Then she slipped the scrap of fabric into the pocket in the notebook cover.

"Oh, look, it's almost four o'clock," Bess said, pointing to her watch. "I told my mother I'd be home by four-fifteen. We'd better get going, guys."

"Well, thanks for showing us the box, Julia," Nancy said. "I'll be sure to let you know when I find some more clues."

"Bye, Mr. Sandback. Bye, Julia," called George and Bess. Then the girls headed home.

That night Nancy sat on her bed. Her chocolate Lab puppy, Chocolate Chip, was nestled against her side. She had her clue notebook in her lap. She looked at the suspect list and crossed out Anderson Quilling's name. Under "Clues" Nancy wrote, "Red felt caught in the gift box. Part of thief's clothes?"

Nancy sighed and patted Chip's head. She couldn't very well go through the closets of everyone who'd been at the Book Nook yesterday. Looking around her room, Nancy's eyes fell on her bookshelf.

"Maybe," Mr. Sandback had said, "there are some clues to be found in that book."

With a shrug Nancy got off the bed and plucked *The Absent Award* from her bookshelf. Sitting at her desk, Nancy began flipping through the first pages of the book. She stopped at a picture of a wooden box.

"Hey, that looks a lot like the box at the Book Nook," she said.

The box was open and empty. Nancy remembered—it had held the award before it was stolen. When Nancy looked at the picture a second time, she gasped.

"I forgot," she said. She quickly read the words on the page next to the picture.

"There!" Nancy said, pointing to the sentence she'd been looking for. Then she read aloud: "'The award absconder had left not a trace. Or so it seemed. But then our wily detective spotted something on the box—a swatch of red felt caught in its hinges.'

"Wow!" Nancy said. "Both boxes had red felt in the hinges. How strange!"

Nancy turned the page. "Maybe Mr. Sandback's right," she said. "Maybe there *are* clues in *The Absent Award.*"

Eagerly, she started to read more. But then Mr. Drew popped his head into her room.

"Nancy," he said, "time for lights-out."

"Okay, Daddy," Nancy said. She shut the book and slipped it into her book bag.

"How's the mystery coming?" Mr. Drew asked as Nancy got into bed. Chip padded to the end of the bed and yawned. Then she flopped down and rested her head on her feet.

"It's too early to tell," Nancy decided, yawning herself. "But after I do more reading tomorrow, maybe I'll have a better idea!"

7

A Clue Hunt

The next morning Nancy couldn't wait to read more of *The Absent Award*. During the math lesson, she got her chance. The bell rang in short bursts. It was a fire drill.

Nancy grabbed her book. Then she walked outside with the rest of her class. All the other kids and teachers in Carl Sandburg Elementary were outside, too. They had to wait fifteen minutes before going back to their classrooms.

As they stood on the front lawn, Nancy opened *The Absent Award* and started to read.

"Ah-ha," Nancy read. "Our wily detective

has spotted another clue. He deduced that the thief had been to an elementary school. How did he make this brilliant deduction, you ask? That careless crook had left something behind on a bench in front of the school. It was a blue leather eye—"

"Hey!" Kyle Leddington's yell caught Nancy's attention. He was standing near a bench near the school's front door. He was waving something in the air.

It was blue.

It was leather.

"I just sat on this thing," Kyle said.

"What is it?" Bess asked.

"It looks like an eyeglass case," Kyle said.

Nancy froze. Then she returned to the sentence she had just read: "It was a blue leather eyeglass case. There was no doubt that it belonged to the terrible award thief."

"Whoa," Nancy whispered. "This is weird."

"Somebody must have lost it," George said.

Kyle threw his head back and yelled, "Did anybody lose a blue eyeglass case?"

Bess glared at Kyle. "I guess he never

heard of the lost-and-found."

But nobody else spoke up.

"I wonder where it came from," Kyle said.

I wonder too! Nancy thought. This is so strange. First I found some red felt, just like the clue in *The Absent Award*. Then this eyeglass case turns up. What next? Maybe the book will tell me.

Quickly, Nancy flipped the pages. In the next chapter the wily detective found his next clue—at a candy store.

"The thief must have had a tremendous sweet tooth," Nancy read. "So intent was he on filling up on sugar, that he didn't notice he had dropped a slip of paper in the candy store. Yes, right between the licorice and the jelly beans. And on this slip of paper were directions to a place. What sort of place it was, the wily detective could not know. But he was sure of one thing—this was where the thief intended to hide the stolen award."

Hmm, Nancy thought when she finished reading. A candy store.

There just happened to be a store right

near Carl Sandburg Elementary. It was called the School Bell. Kids went there to buy school supplies or toys. But the School Bell sold candy, too.

Nancy had a feeling that she'd find more than chocolate at the School Bell today. She turned to Bess and George. "Let's go to the Bell after school today," she suggested.

"The School Bell?" Bess said. "As in candy? Sure! What gave you that idea, Nancy?"

"Well," Nancy said with a little smile, "let's just say I have *another* hunch."

"Finally," Nancy whispered as the last bell of the school day rang.

"Yeah," Bess agreed, putting on her backpack. "Time for candy at the Bell. Let's go!"

The School Bell was an old-fashioned little store filled with everything kids loved. As the girls got near the store, they saw a bunch of third-graders, including Orson Wong, Katie Zaleski, and Andy Nixon.

"Oooh!" George said as they walked through the door. "New soccer balls." She ran over to one of the shelves to have a closer look.

"Soccer!" Bess harrumphed. "Bo-ring. I'm heading for the candy."

"Me, too," Nancy said. She walked to the candy aisle. Lots of kids were already digging into after-school snacks. Josie Blanton, the biggest sweet tooth in the class, was in the chocolate section.

Nancy remembered what she'd read in *The Absent Award*. "The thief left some directions between the licorice and the jelly beans," she whispered to herself.

Nancy headed straight for the jelly beans. Bags of them were hanging from a wire rack. Nancy lifted up each bag to look for a slip of paper. She found nothing.

Frowning, Nancy went to another shelf to look for the licorice. That was when she heard Josie Blanton's voice.

"Hey," Josie said. "Look what I found on top of the Panda Crunch bars."

Nancy ran over to Josie. Josie was gazing curiously at a piece of paper. "Can I see that?" Nancy asked breathlessly.

"Sure," Josie said, handing the paper over. "It looks like a poem."

Nancy peered at the words.

All fouled up?
Searching in vain?
Head downtown on School,
  then Main.
Then a turn on Drake you'll take.
When you find a story—brake!

"These are directions," Nancy cried. "Someone knows where *Foul-up at the Floss Factory* is. That must be why it says, 'All fouled up.'"

"Cool!" George said. "Let's follow the directions."

"Yeah," Nancy said. "We'd better call home for permission."

She turned to the man behind the cash register. He was Mr. Pitt, the School Bell's owner.

"Mr. Pitt," Nancy said. "May we use your phone to call home? It's urgent!"

"Sure, kids," Mr. Pitt said. He handed Bess the cordless phone. As Bess dialed her mother, Orson and Josie walked up.

"What are you doing, Nancy?" Orson asked.

"Following this clue to find Mr. Sandback's missing book," Nancy said.

"Count me in!" Orson said. "Can I use the phone when you're done to get permission?"

A few minutes later all the kids had phoned home. Then Nancy led George, Bess, Josie, and Orson out the door and down School Street.

At the corner of School and Main, Nancy stopped to peer at the poem. "To reach Drake Street, we have to turn right on Main," she said.

"That will take us by the park," George said.

Nancy gasped. She'd had a chance to read more of *The Absent Award* at lunchtime. After the candy store, the wily detective had discovered another clue—a handkerchief— in the park. And after *that,* he'd found a compass in front of the city courthouse.

"We need to stop in the park," she said. "I think we might find another clue there. A handkerchief!"

The kids ran to the park and began hunting for the clue. Josie searched near the swings. George clambered onto the monkey bars to scan the area from high up. Bess peered under the seesaws. Nancy stuffed the slip of paper into her pocket and pawed through some shrubs.

"I don't see anything," she heard Bess call.

"Me, neither," Orson yelled from the sandbox.

Nancy sighed and pushed aside a few spiky branches. "Hmm," she muttered. "Where *is* that hand— Oh!"

Nancy had found something.

Something white.

And soft.

It was a handkerchief! And it was stuck in the branches of the bush.

Holding her breath, Nancy plucked the fabric from the branch. When she examined it, she found three initials stitched in blue onto one corner.

"'M. A. S.,'" Nancy read out loud.

She waved the handkerchief over her head and called to her friends, "Look what I found!"

The kids ran over and Nancy showed them the clue.

"M. A. S.," Bess said. "I wonder whose initials those are."

Suddenly Nancy realized something. She

reached into her book bag and pulled out *The Absent Award*. She turned to the last page and read out loud: "'About the author: Morton Alvin Sandback.'"

"Mr. Sandback's middle name is Alvin," Nancy said.

"Which means that's Mr. Sandback's handkerchief!" George said.

"Why would Mr. Sandback's handkerchief be a clue, though?" Bess asked.

"I'm not sure," Nancy said. "But I think we need to keep searching. The courthouse is on the corner of Main and Drake. Let's go there. According to the book, we're supposed to find a compass there."

The kids walked a block down Main Street until they reached the River Heights courthouse.

They began searching the big courtyard in front of the building. Nancy looked on the courthouse steps. Bess searched the lawn, but Orson Wong just yawned.

"This clue hunt is getting kind of boring," he said. He walked over to the flagpole and began spinning around it. He spun faster and faster until he got dizzy.

"Ugh," he yelled, grabbing the flag rope so he wouldn't fall down.

Nancy glanced at Orson and rolled her eyes. Then she looked again. Orson was peering at something attached to the end of the flag rope. Then he took the thing off and waved it in the air.

"The clue!" Orson yelled. "I think I found the clue!"

Nancy ran over to Orson. He showed her a pencil. Instead of an eraser on top, there was a little round dial.

George peeked at the instrument. "It's a compass!" she said. "My dad and I used one on our last camping trip."

"Look," Nancy said. "It has a little mark on it."

Nancy squinted at the compass. There was a tiny red X on the dial, right over the W.

"According to this compass, we're supposed to go west on Drake Street," she said. "Maybe the next thing we'll find is Mr. Sandback's book!"

8

Suspect: Sandback?

Nancy and her friends headed west down Drake Street.

"I wonder where this clue will take us," Bess said excitedly.

"I don't know," Nancy said, fishing the slip of paper out of her pocket. "The directions say, 'When you find a story—brake!' I wonder what that means?"

The group tromped down Drake Street for a half block.

Then another half block.

And then another whole block!

"I don't see anything," George said.

"Neither do I," Nancy answered.

A block farther Drake Street hit a dead end.

"Oh, no!" Nancy cried. "Where do we go now?"

She looked up.

And then she gasped.

"It's the Book Nook!" she said. "I didn't even realize it. 'When you see a story— brake!' The Book Nook is *full* of stories. The compass and the directions were leading us right to it."

"Let's go inside," Josie said.

The kids ran up the stairs and into the bookstore. The first person they saw was Mr. Sandback. He was sitting behind the front desk. His long, skinny arms were folded across his chest. He was wearing his familiar big grin and his black vest with all the funny patches.

"Hello, children," he said. He didn't seem very surprised to see them. "Have you found the missing book yet?"

"Well," Nancy said, "we found a lot of clues, and they led us here, to the Book Nook."

"I wonder why," Mr. Sandback said.

Suddenly, clue after clue fell into place in Nancy's mind.

"I think I know why," she burst out. "And I think I know who the thief is."

"Really?" Mr. Sandback said. "Do tell!"

"But . . . it doesn't make sense at all," Nancy said. Her forehead crinkled in a confused frown. "Because, Mr. Sandback, I think the thief is you."

"What!" exclaimed all the other kids.

Mr. Sandback didn't look angry. In fact, he looked as if someone had just told him a wonderful joke.

"I'm the thief?" he asked. "Why do you say that, Detective Drew?"

"The clues all point to you," Nancy said. She reached into her book bag and pulled out all the things she and her friends had found.

"I found this piece of red felt in the hinges of the box that the book was stolen from," Nancy said. She pulled the bit of fabric from her clue notebook and showed it to Mr. Sandback. Then she pointed to a red typewriter on Mr. Sandback's vest. Part of the patch was ripped away.

"It looks like the felt came from that patch!" Nancy exclaimed.

Next she pointed to the half-moons propped on Mr. Sandback's nose. "You wear glasses," she said.

She held out the case that Kyle had found on the bench in front of the school. "So, maybe this blue leather eyeglass case belongs to you."

Mr. Sandback nodded. "Go on," he said.

Feeling more confused than ever, Nancy showed Mr. Sandback the handkerchief she'd found in the bush.

"Your middle name is Alvin, which makes your initials M. A. S.," she said. "And those are exactly the initials on this handkerchief."

"Hey, what about the pencil, I found?" Orson said.

"Remember what Mr. Sandback said here on Sunday," Nancy pointed out.

"I always write with a good old-fashioned *pencil,*" Mr. Sandback said. "Nancy, you've found me out."

With that, Mr. Sandback reached beneath the front desk and pulled out a ragged copy of *Foul-up at the Floss Factory.*

"The first edition!" George exclaimed. "You had it all the time!"

"But why would you steal your own book?" Nancy said.

Just then Nancy heard the click of a door opening behind her. She turned around to see Julia coming out of the office. She was wearing a grin much like her father's. Behind her was Anderson Quilling. He was smiling, too.

"I see you reached the bottom of the mystery," she said. "You see, Nancy, this was another one of Dad's little pranks."

"I thought it would be fun to bring one of my mysteries to life," Mr. Sandback said. "So I re-created *The Absent Award* for my fans to solve. And you did a bang-up job, Nancy!"

"My friends helped with the clue hunt, too," Nancy said.

"I warned you," Julia said, placing a hand on Nancy's shoulder. "My father has lots of tricks up his sleeve."

"Were you in on it, Julia?" Nancy asked.

"Yup!" Julia said. "And so was Anderson, here. And Mrs. Goldstein. We thought it

would be a fun game for you all."

"So," Mr. Sandback said, turning to the small crowd of kids in front of the desk, "did you enjoy the mystery?"

"Yeah!" Nancy and her friends shouted.

"And most of all," Nancy added, "I'm glad you have your rare book."

"Well, actually," Mr. Sandback said, patting the book cover fondly, "I thought I'd donate this book to the River Heights Public Library. They could put it on display for all readers to see—not just me."

"That's so nice, Mr. Sandback!" Bess said.

"And it may not end there," Mr. Sandback said. He gazed down at Nancy with another big grin. "I have a feeling Nancy Drew might see her name in my next mystery story, *The Crook Who Took the Book*."

"Wow!" Nancy said. "Thanks, Mr. Sandback!"

While her friends crowded around the famous author, Nancy picked up her clue notebook and pulled a pencil from her book bag. She sat in a chair and opened her notebook to the "Missing Mystery" page. Then she wrote:

Not only did I get to meet my favorite author, I got to solve one of his mysteries. It just goes to show that Mr. Sandback was right—there are adventures all around us. You just have to know where to look. And sometimes, the best place to look is in a book!

Case closed.

HITTY'S TRAVELS #1: Civil War Days

Hitty's owner, Nell, lives on a plantation in North Carolina. When a house slave named Sarina comes to work for Nell's father, the girls become friends. But when Nell and Sarina break the rules of the plantation, things will never be the same again. . . .

HITTY'S TRAVELS #2: Gold Rush Days

Hitty's owner, Annie, is excited to travel with her father to California in search of gold, but it's a tough journey out West and an even tougher life when they arrive. Annie longs to help out, but is there anything she can do?

HITTY'S TRAVELS #3: Voting Rights Days

Hitty's owner, Emily, lives in Washington, D.C. Emily's aunt Ada and many other women are trying to win the right to vote. But when the women are put in jail, all hope seems lost. Will Emily—and Hitty—find a way to help the cause?

HITTY'S TRAVELS #4: Ellis Island Days

Hitty travels to Italy in style with a spoiled little rich girl, but soon falls into the hands of Fiorella Rossi, a kind girl whose poor family longs to reach America. Will the Rossis survive the awful conditions of their long journey?

Available from Aladdin Paperbacks
Published by Simon & Schuster